Something for Mother

by Laura Alden
illustrated by Linda Hohag

created by Wing Park Publishers

 CHILDRENS PRESS®
CHICAGO

Library of Congress Cataloging-in-Publication Data

Alden, Laura, 1955-
 Something for Mother / by Laura Alden ; illustrated by Linda Hohag ;
created by Wing Park Publishers.
  p.   cm. — (Circle the year with holidays)
 Summary: Andrea and her friends plant flowers in an old wagon to
surprise their mothers on Mother's Day. Includes instructions for
games, songs, and crafts.
  ISBN 0-516-00690-8 (library binding)
  [1.Mother's Day—Fiction.   2. Handicraft.]   I. Hohag, Linda,
ill.   II. Wing Park Publishers.   III. Title.   IV. Series.
PZ7.A3586So   1994
[E]—dc20   93-37096
                                                        CIP
                                                        AC

Something for Mother

"Andrea," said her mother softly. "Here's
your sleeping pal. She's fallen out of bed."

Andrea felt fur against her neck. It was Silky,
her stuffed seal pup.

"Morning," said Andrea sleepily. She stroked
Silky's grey fur.

"Time to get up, honey," her mother said.
"You don't want to miss the bus."
Andrea heard rain outside. She got up and
carefully tucked Silky back under the covers.

Soon Andrea was splashing through the puddles.

"Hi, Anne. Hi, Mark," she called as she hurried to the bus. The twins lived next door.

After Andrea, Anne, and Mark were seated
on the bus, E.T., Nora, Joseph, and Ross got on.
"Yuk!" said Nora. "What a rainy day!"
"Yeah," Ross agreed. "I wonder if Mr. Parks
will let us go outside."

"Mr. Parks said something about planning special Mother's Day projects today," said Andrea.

"I wonder what they will be," said Anne.

"I want to do something really special for my mom," Andrea said, as they pulled up to the school.

"It is early to be planning for Mother's Day," Mr. Parks told them when class began. "We are starting now because I am putting you into groups of six or seven, and each group is to come up with its own ideas for Mother's Day this year."

Everyone started talking at once. "Settle down!" called Mr. Parks. "I'll give you some time to talk about it. First, think about what your mothers would like," he said.

The children sat in small circles to talk.

"My mother likes perfume," said Joseph.

"My mom wants a computer," Nora said.

"How about baskets?" asked Ross. "My mother likes baskets."

"Cookies!" shouted E.T. "Let's make cookies!"

11

Mr. Parks walked over. "Now, E.T., you're
the one who likes cookies. Try to think what
your mom would like. Maybe you could fix
her breakfast in bed."

"Flowers," said Andrea suddenly. "They would all like flowers."

"Yeah," said Anne. "We could grow flowers."

"That will take some time," said Mr. Parks.
"You could work on it as part of our unit on
Growing Things."

"Where will we plant the garden?" asked Joseph, as Mr. Parks left to go help another group.

Andrea wondered that, too.

Andrea sat on the steps after school, watching her little brother, Sammy, play in the sandbox. "Where could we put our garden?" she said out loud.

Sammy was dumping sand into Andrea's old, red wagon. It was full of sand and dirt and even a few weeds.

Andrea looked at the weeds. Hmmm . . . She
took Sammy inside to Mother and ran next
door to talk with her friends.

"You want to plant the garden in your old wagon?" asked Anne.

"A garden on wheels!" Mark shouted. "Yes, that sounds like fun!"

"I agree," said Anne. "Andrea, let's go talk to your mom."

"Sure you can take your old wagon to school," said Andrea's mother. "In fact, I'll help you."

Andrea's mom helped her empty the sand from the wagon.

Andrea was so excited she could hardly stand still. Her mom had no idea it was for a Mother's Day project. All Andrea said was, "Okay. Thanks, Mom."

The next day, Andrea's mom brought the wagon to school.

Mr. Parks brought tiny marigold plants for the group and potting soil, too. The children poked holes in the bottom of the wagon so the soil wouldn't get too wet. Every day they worked at their project.

"I still think making cookies would have been better," said E.T.

The next few weeks, the children took turns caring for their garden. They weeded and watered it, wheeling it into the sunshine each morning.

Because of their work and care, the flowers grew. Even E.T. got excited.

Then, it was the Friday before Mother's Day.

Mr. Parks took the wagon with the flowers to Andrea's house. Andrea's dad helped hide it in the garage.

"Let's deliver the flowers together," said Nora.

"But each of us chooses which marigolds to pick," said Ross.

Mother's Day morning was sunny and warm. The friends gathered early on Andrea's front steps. Andrea knocked on her own door.

Her mother answered the door. "Happy Mother's Day!" the children shouted. Andrea gave her mother a bouquet from their garden on wheels.

"Surprise! I love you," she said. Then she gave her mother a hug.

"Oh, Andrea!" said her mother, hugging her
back. "Thank you! So that's what you wanted
the wagon for. What a surprise—and what a
beautiful gift!" And she waved to the children
as they rolled their garden next door and down
the block.

MOTHER'S DAY FUN WITH LEARNING

If desired, continue the theme of the book by planting a garden in your classroom. One idea is to use an old wagon, wheelbarrow or child's toy with wheels. Prepare the container by poking drainage holes in the bottom. Then help children fill it with potting soil. Try some potted plants (parsley, beans, pansies, petunias) and seeds (lettuce, radishes, marigolds, nasturtiums) in between the plants. Have children care for the garden as it grows.

Another idea (which could also be used for a Mother's Day gift) is to have each child plant a flower in the bottom of a two-liter plastic soda bottle. (Use those with separate round bottoms.) Remove bottle from bottom, cut off top fourth of bottle (including spout and neck) and place remaining dome upside down on bottom container. Makes a miniature greenhouse!

More Mother's Day Fun

1. Things to Create:

To send home for Mother's Day or to give at a "Mother's Day Tea": Provide each child with two copies of a simple paper outline of a teapot. Have children hinge the copies together with glue or a staple and decorate the front cover with paint or markers. On the inside, write or have them write:

"When you've had a long, long day
And you're tired, so you say—
I will try to let you be
So you can have this cup of tea!"

Children can paste a teabag inside to provide the tea and sign their names.

Or: Have children make their mothers or grand-mothers a special place to keep special treasures, pictures and letters. Have each bring in a shoe box and cover the box with gift wrap, stickers or construction paper, especially illustrated by the child. Encourage children to place a set of love tokens in the box. The handmade tokens can promise cooperation, hugs and kisses, specific chores or special treatment (such as breakfast in bed).

2. Things to Do:

Play a relay—"How Does Your Garden Grow?" Divide players into teams of five. Place three small paper cups, each containing a spoonful of potting soil, several yards in front of each team. Give the following roles and materials to each team: "Sower"— three large seeds; "Soil"—a container full of soil and a spoon; "Rain"—small can of water; "Sprout"—five strips of green paper; "Gardener"—garden gloves. Upon a "go" signal, "Sower" runs up and places one seed in each cup, returns and touches "Soil" who runs to cover each planting with a spoonful of soil. "Rain" waters each seed. "Sprout" "plants" the paper strips. "Gardener" pulls up the strips before running back home.

Play "Mother, May I?"

Dress-up or charades. Have children dress-up as and enact the various roles that mothers and fathers have. Children of the opposite sex can do the guessing.

3. Things to Share:

Learn one or more of the following songs/fingerplays:

Happy Mother's Day

(Sung to the tune of Mary Had a Little Lamb.)
Mothers, grandmas, we love you,
We love you, we love you,
Neighbors, aunts and teachers, too—
Happy Mother's Day to you!

—Laura Alden

Mother, I Love You So!

(Sung to the tune of Twinkle, Twinkle, Little Star)
Mother, just to let you know,
   (shake pointer finger)
I will say I love you so.
   (throw a kiss)
Though I'm sometimes cross or loud,
   (wave arms and stamp feet)
I will try to make you proud.
   (put thumbs under armpits as if hooked in suspenders)
Mother, just to let you know,
   (shake pointer finger)
I will say I love you so.
   (throw a kiss)

4. More Things to Do:

Observation and memory game: "Mom's Pock-etbook." Select items commonly found in a woman's purse—comb, mirror, pen, coin purse, handkerchief, etc. In small groups, have children look at the items, then close their eyes as one child takes an item or two away. Children name what is missing.

Sequencing and storytelling: Provide pictures of scenes in a woman's day (from women's home and professional magazines) for children to put in sequence.

Comparing and contrasting: Have children bring in two photos—one showing them with their mothers when they were babies and current pictures of themselves and their mothers. Allow children to match the photos. Matching grandmothers with grandchildren may provide even more of a challenge.